THE JOYFUL Book

TODD PARR

Megan Tingley Books
LITTLE, BROWN AND COMPANY
NEW YORK BOSTON

TO THE WORLD

Also by Todd Parr

A complete list of Todd's books and more information can be found at toddparr.com.

About This Book

The illustrations for this book were created on a drawing tablet using an iMac, starting with bold black lines and dropping in color with Adobe Photoshop. This book was edited by Megan Tingley and Esther Cajahuaringa and designed by Lynn El-Roeiy. The production was supervised by Patricia Alvarado, and the production editor was Marisa Finkelstein. The text was set in Todd Parr's signature font.

Feeling joyful is when you are so happy you want to jump and shout with everyone you love.

Celebrating with family and friends is joyful.

Going on vacation is joyful.

Unwrapping presents is joyful.

Lighting candles is joyful.

Storytelling is joyful.

Trying new things is joyful.

Having company over is joyful.

Watching a parade is joyful.

Rubbing noses is joyful.

Getting dressed up is joyful.

Giving is joyful.

Singing holiday songs is joyful.

Playing games is joyful.

Hugging is joyful.

friends far away is joyful.

Sharing a meal is joyful.

Playing outside is joyful.

Learning new traditions is joyful.

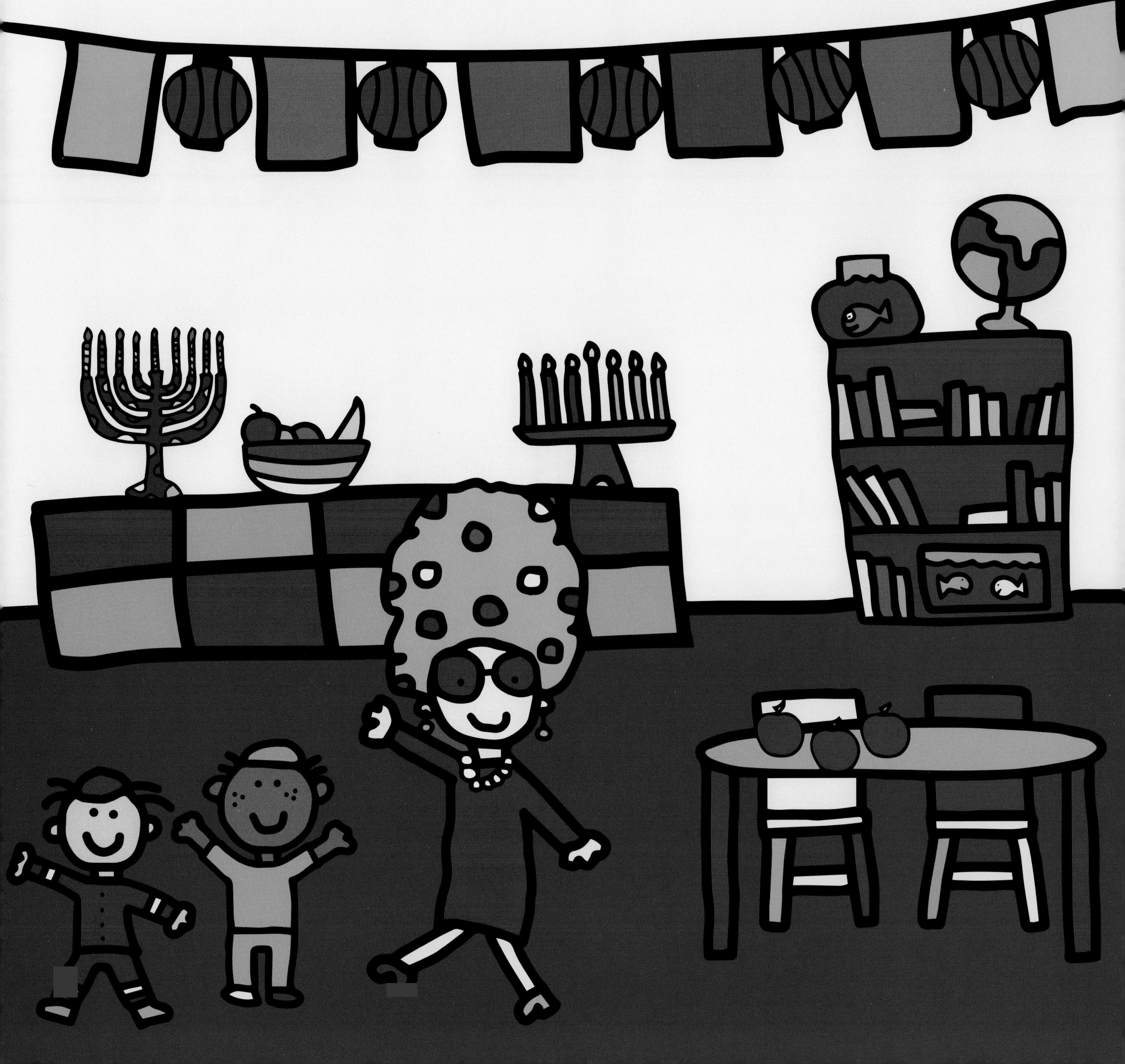

Making yummy treats is joyful.

Visiting friends is joyful.

Decorating for the holidays is joyful.

Saying thank you is joyful.

Starting a new year is joyful!

Holidays are a special time. No matter what traditions you celebrate, it is always joyful to be together with family and friends. Try to find joy every day and share it with others all year long! The end. Love, Todd